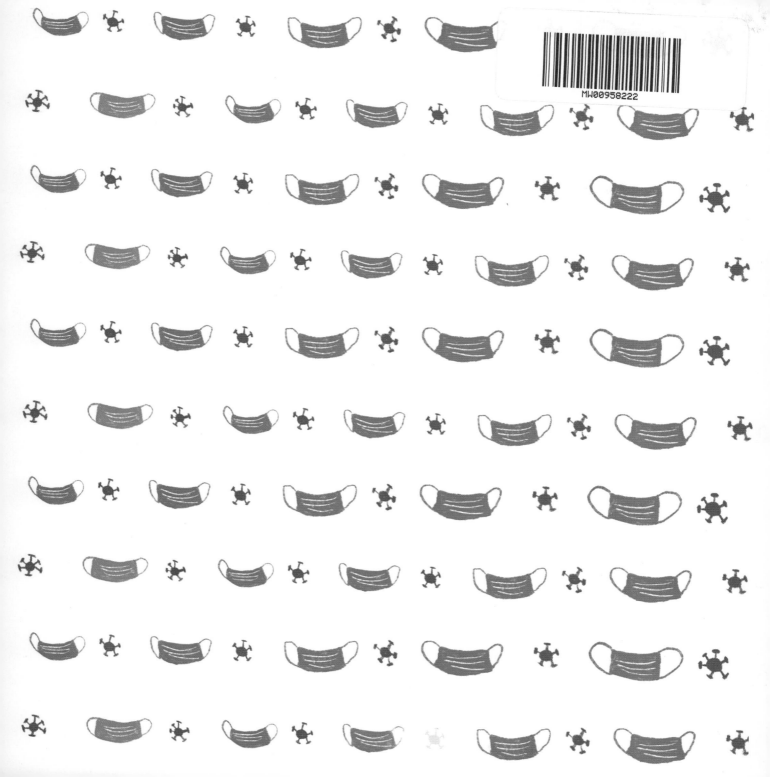

To Adriana, Rayan and Ramsey
You taught me to smile with my eyes even when things were
difficult. Thank you for always reminding me that there's light to
be found in every moment, even the darker ones.
S. S.

To Chad and Adam
Life is unpredictable; never miss an opportunity to hug and kiss.
There is no such thing as too much love.
K. J.

THE EXTRAORDINARY
PAUSE

BY SARA SADIK
ILLUSTRATED BY KARINE JABER

Eifrig Publishing LLC

Lemont   Berlin

Not long ago in a land we all know, things were moving fast.

So fast that everyone stopped noticing the
smell of fresh pancakes,

and the color green,

and even each other.

And it was in *that* moment
that a virus arrived.

It visited every corner...

of every country...

even though it wasn't invited.

And because it was so unexpected and unknown,
the world hit pause.

and stayed
home.

The world changed overnight.

Schools were closed.

Restaurants were emptied.

Birthday parties were postponed.

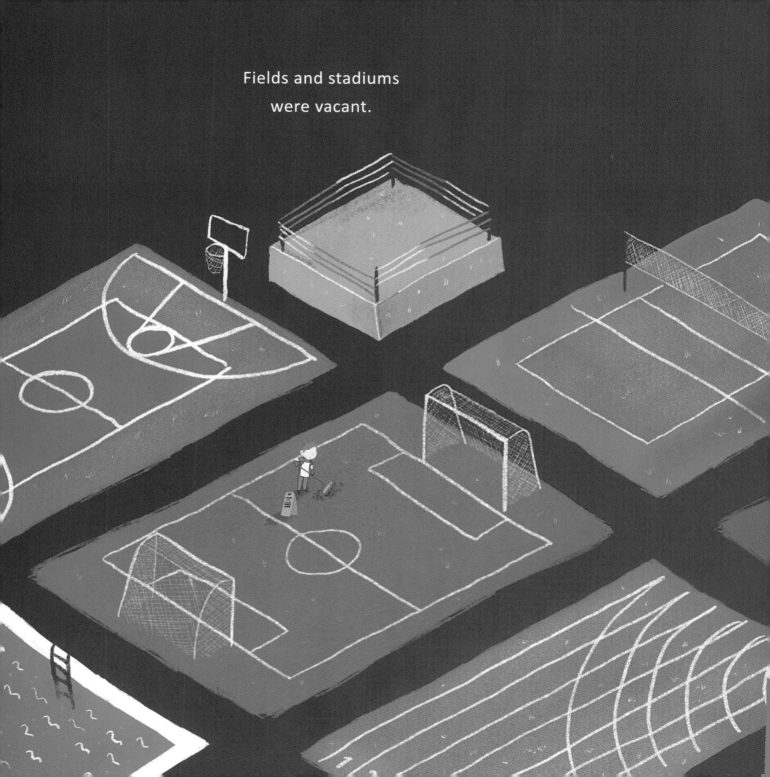

Fields and stadiums
were vacant.

Ice cream parlors were deserted.

And all the world's
swings, seesaws,
and slides were abandoned.

People were forced to look through binoculars, photographs, and their imaginations to remember what life looked like.

Hugs were forbidden!

Kisses were illegal.

And holding hands and high-fives? A HUGE no-no!

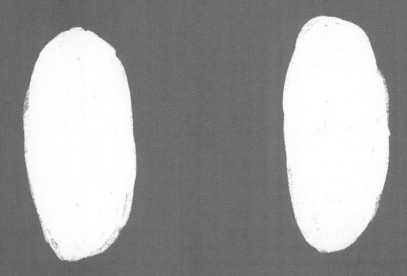

The virus felt like a big old bully—
mean, scary, and unfair.

Inside, things were different too.

.

For some,
life s-l-o-w-e-d down,

while for many others,
it had never moved faster.

People felt and found things
they had forgotten.
And when their masks
hid their faces,
they smiled with their eyes.

Mommies taught math.
Daddies taught reading.

Home became the center of it all.

Teachers and classmates all waved from a screen.

At least at home, kisses weren't illegal
and hugs were always welcome!

Before anyone knew it,
days and weeks turned into months
and even years.

It all seemed to blur together——

that long and endless pause.

But we eventually realized:
sometimes it *takes* a pause
to bring it all back.

Like the smell of fresh pancakes,

and the color green,

and the moments where we *really* notice each other.

How did your life change during the extraordinary pause?

What changed during the pandemic:

    in your family?

    with friends?

    at school?

    in your community?

What good thing happened that was unexpected?

How did the pandemic change your ideas about:

    connecting with others?

    health and safety?

    attending school?

What did you miss most?

What are you most grateful for now?

What was the hardest part about living through a pandemic?

What did you learn during the pandemic that you will take with you into the future?

Scan for additional resources

A special thank you to all first responders, grocery store workers, teachers, caretakers, farmers, factory and sanitation workers who work so hard to support and protect us.

Sara Sadik, Author

An optimist at heart, Sara tries to see the silver lining in the darkest situations. This was put to the test during the pandemic and in the many challenges of homeschooling three kids ages 3-6. This idea for this book developed in between lockdowns, dance-offs, and COVID-testing. When she is not writing, Sara is a public speaker and works to promote reading and writing to children in the Middle East.

Karine Jaber, Illustrator

Juggling life balance is something Karine is used to. Mom of two young boys, full time creative director, graphic designer and illustrator, she found in quarantine a time to breathe and take a step back from the routine and chaos of a 9-to-5 job. Despite the fear and uncertainties that came during the pandemic, she can now say that she learned a lesson or two from the resilience of her kids and recognizes the importance of appreciating the moment.

Published by Eifrig Publishing,
PO Box 66, Lemont, PA 16851, USA
Knobelsdorffstr. 44, 14059 Berlin, Germany.

For information regarding permission, write to:
Rights and Permissions Department,
Eifrig Publishing,
PO Box 66, Lemont, PA 16851, USA.
permissions@eifrigpublishing.com, +1-814-954-9445

Library of Congress Control Number: 2021942445

  Sadik, Sara
The Extraordinary Pause/
by Sara Sadik, illustrated by Karine Jaber,
edited by Jason Gruhl
p. cm.

Paperback: ISBN 978-1-63233-306-3
Hard cover: ISBN 978-1-63233-307-0
Ebook: ISBN 978-1-63233-305-6

[1. Pandemic – Juvenile Fiction. 2. Family – Juvenile Fiction.]

I. Jaber, Karine, ill. II. Title: The Extraordinary Pause

25 24 23 22 2021
5 4 3 2 1

Printed in UAE on paper from sustainable forests